The Miracle in Bethlehem

The Miracle in Bethlehem

A Storyteller's Tale

Sarah Burton

Illustrated by Katriona Chapman

Floris Books

Published in 2008 by Floris Books

British Library CIP Data available

ISBN 978-086315-663-2

Printed in Poland

For

Thomas

Angus

Joseph

Jacob

and Ruby

Once upon a time, perhaps two thousand years ago, or maybe only yesterday, a man stood under a tree and waited.

The tree was very old and very big, as broad as it was tall, and shaded the man from the sun. It would be difficult to say how old the man was. When his face was round and smiling, he looked almost like a child, but when he was being serious or sad, he looked more like an extremely wise old man.

His clothes gave no clue as to what he was. A long cloak of patchwork covered him from head to toe. Only a rich person, some people said, could afford all those different materials and pay someone to spend days sewing them all together. Only a poor person, others said, would make a coat of patches, or have the time to make it. It was a mystery.

On his head he wore a small round black hat, which no one had ever seen him take off. In his hand he carried a long stick made of ebony, carved with people and animals and birds and fruit and flowers. The more you looked at that stick, the more different pictures you could see in it.

As he waited, people began to arrive: old people, young people, children, parents with babies, and even a couple of dogs. They settled on the cool grass under the shade of the great tree. As the number of people grew, some of the children climbed into the lower branches of the tree to get a better view of the Storyteller, for that is who the man was.

Once a year, everyone gathered round to hear him tell this story.

When he was satisfied that everyone who was going to come had arrived and was sitting comfortably, this is how he began:

'Our story begins in Jerusalem,' said the Storyteller, 'in the days of the Roman Empire. Caesar Augustus was in power in Rome, a long way away.

'Now, ruling the world is more than any single man can handle, even if he is a god, as Caesar considered himself to be. So the various kingdoms of Caesar's empire were ruled by regional governors. Here, in Jerusalem, the regional governor was King Herod.

'Herod was a local man, loyal to the Empire. He was doing a good job and the Emperor had no complaints.

'Herod was a busy man, of course, and at the particular moment we are interested in, he was busier than usual. Caesar Augustus had ordered a census. Having conquered the world, he wanted to know just how much it was worth. Every man, woman and child had to be counted and registered.

'That's a lot of paperwork. And just when he least needed it, Herod discovered he'd got another little problem.'

Herod looked up from his papers. It was late and he was tired.

'Marcus!' he called. 'What *is* that noise outside?'

Marcus turned from the window. A veteran of many Roman campaigns, he was now Herod's right-hand man.

'Looks like you've got visitors, sir,' he informed Herod.

'Visitors? At this time of night?' Herod sighed. 'Go down and tell them to come back in the morning.'

'Very good, sir,' said Marcus, and marched smartly out. Almost immediately, he returned. 'I think perhaps you'd better see them, sir.'

'What?' Herod asked irritably, engrossed again in his papers.

'They look sort of ...' Marcus's voice trailed away. 'I think they might be ...'

'Do spit it out, Marcus,' snapped Herod.

'Kings, sir,' said Marcus.

Herod thought for a moment.

'How many?' he asked.

'Three, sir.'

'Where are they from?'

'Afar,' said Marcus.

'Afar? Where's that?'

'A long way away. Persia, I think, sir,' said Marcus.

'Persia, eh?' Herod was thoughtful.

'Yes, sir,' said Marcus. 'Where the carpets come from,' he added helpfully.

'I know that!' said Herod. Marcus was always telling him things he already knew. But sometimes Marcus would tell him something he didn't know and for a man in Herod's position all information was valuable. 'I suppose you'd better show them in,' he said wearily.

The visitors were brought in and in turn bowed before Herod. One had a large roll of paper under his arm. Another carried a book. The third carried a bag which Herod hoped might contain presents. Herod liked presents.

'And whom have I the pleasure of addressing?' Herod asked politely. Experience had taught him it was wise to be courteous to royalty. He was, after all, a king himself.

'I am Caspar,' said the first.

'I am Melchior,' said the second.

'I am Balthazar,' said the third.

Herod extended his hand to Caspar. 'And you are king of ...?'

'Oh, we're not really kings,' Caspar said quickly. Herod snatched back his hand.

'Not as you know them,' added Melchior.

Herod looked sharply at Marcus. Marcus shrugged his shoulders.

'Well, what are you then?' Herod asked the men.

'We are magi, King Herod,' explained Balthazar.

'That's wise men, sir,' Marcus whispered.

'I know what magi are, Marcus,' Herod hissed back. He considered Balthazar. 'And how may I help you?'

Balthazar unrolled the large piece of thick paper he was carrying and showed it to Herod. It was a map of the sky.

'A new star has appeared in the East …' Melchior said.

'Brighter than all the others in the heavens …' Caspar interrupted.

'And we are following it,' explained Balthazar.

They all seemed very excited about the star, but Herod was waiting for them to get to the point.

Marcus stepped in. 'They're tracking its trajectory, sir,' he explained. 'This exceptionally bright star — they're watching it to see where it will go.'

Herod stared uncomprehendingly at Marcus. Marcus just shrugged again. They were magi after all. They probably had their reasons. Then a light dawned in Herod's mind. They wanted money. He explained that he understood that they would need provisions — equipment, perhaps — for their journey. And he explained that while Rome was always pleased to encourage new learning, new discoveries, and so forth, budgets were tight. He couldn't promise to fund every little project that was brought before him, although of course he would like to. 'I'll see what I can do,' he said, and began to walk towards the door. The audience was over.

'We ask nothing of you, King Herod,' Caspar said.

'We thought you would want to know about the star because of the prophecy.' Balthazar's clear voice rang round the hall.

Herod stopped in his tracks. 'The prophecy?' he repeated, looking searchingly at Marcus. But Marcus's face told him nothing.

'Ah, yes, the prophecy,' said Herod, who was not a stupid man. 'How does it go again?'

'The people that walked in darkness have seen a great light,' Caspar began to quote. *'They that dwell in the land of the shadow of death, upon them hath the light shined.'*

Herod looked a little disappointed. He'd heard this kind of thing before and it hadn't made any sense then either.

'For unto us a child is born, unto us a son is given,' Balthazar continued, *'and the government shall be upon his shoulders …'*

At the word 'government', Herod pricked up his ears.

'… and his name shall be Wonderful,' Balthazar went on, *'Counsellor, the Mighty God, the everlasting Father, the Prince of Peace.'*

'Of the increase of his government and peace there shall be no end …' added Melchior.

'No end?' Herod repeated.

'… upon the throne of David, and upon his kingdom, to order it, and establish it with judgement and with justice henceforth even for ever.'

By the time Melchior had finished Herod was seriously concerned. There was no doubt: David's kingdom meant the kingdom of the Jews — Herod's subjects. He took Marcus aside.

'I don't like the sound of this prince one bit,' he said.

'No, sir,' agreed Marcus. 'Sounds like a trouble-maker, sir.'

Indeed, the last thing Herod needed was for the people he governed to start believing that someone else was their true leader. How would Herod keep order? What would the Emperor say? Or do?

Herod turned back to the visitors. 'What's all this got to do with your star?' he asked.

Balthazar tapped the book Caspar was holding. 'Another prophecy tells us that the ruler of Israel will appear in Bethlehem.'

'The star is travelling in that precise direction,' Caspar explained.

'You see, my lord?' said Melchior. 'Everything fits.'

'Everything fits,' repeated Herod thoughtfully. Again he took Marcus aside. 'What do you think?' he asked the old soldier. 'We've had false alarms before. Does this strike you as authentic?'

'The magi are usually pretty reliable, sir,' said Marcus.

When Herod turned back to face the visitors he was smiling. 'Thank you for bringing me this joyful news,' he said. 'I would be extremely grateful if, when you find this ...' — he swallowed hard — '... prince ... you would immediately inform me of his whereabouts so that I too may come and ...' — he cleared his throat — '... worship him.'

The magi bowed and were gone with as little ceremony as they had arrived. As soon as the door closed behind them the smile fell from Herod's lips. 'Marcus, this has to be handled just right,' he said urgently, and started pacing about. 'We cannot tolerate any challenge to the authority of Rome. If the magi believe this is the man they've been waiting for, the people will too. This so-called prince must be eliminated. Do you understand?'

'Nip it in the bud, sir,' Marcus agreed.

'Exactly. Assemble your men now. You must leave at once.'

Marcus turned on his heel and marched — again smartly — out of the hall, leaving Herod alone with his thoughts. But Marcus was soon back again.

'I'm sorry, sir,' he said, 'but I forgot to ask. What will he look like? I mean, how will we identify him?'

'I think you'll know,' Herod replied. 'When you see him you'll know he's the one.'

Finally Herod was alone. With a slight shiver of regret he realized the gifts the magi brought were not for him after all.

'Now we must go back nine months,' said the Storyteller, and he swung his cloak like a magician as if he were really turning back time.

'Nine months earlier,' he said, 'in the town of Nazareth, there was a girl called Mary. Mary was just an ordinary child ...'

Somebody had started talking. Someone else said 'Shhhh!' and the Storyteller continued: 'Mary, as I said, was just an ordinary girl ...'

But the talking continued. 'I'm sorry,' said the Storyteller, a little impatiently. 'Is there a problem?'

'Yes,' said a voice. Everyone turned and looked. A woman with red hair had stood up. 'Yes, actually there *is* a problem.'

'Hear, hear,' said a woman wearing a green necklace.

'Mary was *not* an ordinary child,' said Red Hair.

'Certainly not,' agreed Green Beads.

'I beg your pardon,' said the Storyteller, 'but the whole point of Mary is that she was ordinary! It could have been you or me — well, not me, obviously, but an ordinary girl. The whole point is that she *wasn't* special!'

'I've never heard such rubbish,' said Red Hair. 'Mary had *always* been a special child and *that's* the whole point.'

The two women picked their way through the audience, trying not to step on people's hands and feet, and the Storyteller, who was not a little embarrassed, was obliged to give way to them. 'Excuse *me,*' he said huffily.

Red Hair and Green Beads politely inclined their heads to him in thanks and then ignored him completely.

'As I said,' Red Hair told the listeners, 'Mary had always been a special child. You see, her parents couldn't have children, which made them very sad ...'

'*Very* sad,' emphasized Green Beads. 'And Anna …'

'That's Mary's mother —' added Red Hair, 'prayed and prayed …'

'And prayed and prayed …'

'And prayed and prayed — and suddenly an angel appeared.'

The listeners gasped.

'Anna, Anna, the Lord has heard your prayer,' said Green Beads, in the sort of voice she thought an angel might have. *'You shall conceive and bear. Your child shall be spoken of in the whole world.'*

'And then Anna made a promise,' said Red Hair.

'As the Lord my God lives,' said Green Beads, being Anna now, *'if I bear a child, whether male or female, I will bring it as a gift to the Lord my God, and it shall serve him all the days of its life.'*

'Anna did have a baby and Mary was born,' said the Storyteller quickly, 'and Anna kept her part of the bargain. When Mary was only a tiny little girl Anna took her to work and live in the Temple, and she remained there until she was sixteen and it was time to find her a husband.'

'But I don't *want* to get married!' said Mary, pulling away from Anna.

The Temple was almost empty. Some women were singing somewhere.

Anna caught her daughter by the arm. 'Mary, listen to me. Ever since you were a baby …'

'I know! I know I was a special baby!' Mary was almost shouting: she'd heard it all a hundred times before. 'But I don't *want* to be special. I want to be … just … normal.'

'Of course you do,' Anna soothed her, putting her arms round her. Mary stopped struggling and sobbed into her mother's shoulder. 'But it's not all about *us* and what *we* want, is it?'

That night, Mary was allowed to sleep at home, because she was soon to be married. To whom, she did not yet know. 'Tell me about when I was little,' she said.

Anna sat down on the bed and smoothed the hair off Mary's forehead. 'You were only three years old when I took you to the Temple, as I had promised. You were a darling child — irresistible. Even the priest had to pick you up and kiss you. He said …'

'The Lord has magnified your name among all generations. (Mary knew the priest's words off by heart.) *Because of you, the Lord at the end of the days will reveal his redemption to the sons of Israel.'*

And Mary fell asleep, because although the priest's words made her feel apprehensive, they were also, in a way, comforting.

'Yes, but what did it mean?' asked one of the children.

'It meant that Mary was born as part of a big plan to save us all,' said Green Beads. 'It was her destiny.'

The Storyteller was about to speak.

'*Anyway,*' said Red Hair. 'The priest put little Mary down in front of the altar and Anna expected she would be shy …'

'Or afraid,' chipped in Green Beads.

'Well, you know what children are.'

'So what *did* she do?' asked the Storyteller, a little impatiently.

'She danced!' they said together.

'She danced on the steps of the altar,' said Green Beads.

'And everybody *marvelled,*' said Red Hair.

'Well, if you're quite finished —' began the Storyteller.

'So Mary entered the Temple of the Lord,' Red Hair ploughed on, 'where she was nurtured like a dove, and received food from the hand of an angel.'

At this last detail the Storyteller gave Red Hair a hard look.

'May I continue?' he asked. The two women smiled graciously at him. 'Now, where was I? Ah, yes. Mary was sixteen, and it was time to find her a husband. Now, Joseph was an old man …' here the Storyteller dared the women to interrupt him, '… of, perhaps, forty years of age. His trade was carpentry …' Here, Red Hair was about to say something, but the Storyteller was prepared. 'Though *some say* that he was quite a substantial building contractor, with many employees. He was a bachelor …' Here, Green Beads opened her mouth, but again the Storyteller anticipated her. 'Though *some say* he was a widower with grown-up children.' Green Beads closed her mouth.

'At any rate,' the Storyteller continued, 'Joseph was a carpenter and a simple man. He was quite content with his lot, was generous to the Temple, and certainly had no intention of getting married.'

'Again,' said Green Beads.

'But I don't want to get married!' said Joseph as the priest — the same priest that Mary had danced before on the altar steps thirteen years before — led him into the Temple.

'Just stand there, please,' said the priest.

There were four men already there. One was Joseph's friend Jacob, an olive grower. Then there was Joachim, who made sandals. Joseph only knew the other two by sight. They all looked rather miserable. Mary was also there. Joseph didn't know her personally, but everybody knew she was 'special', and that her specialness was part of a big plan — what the plan was exactly, no one seemed sure. She also looked rather miserable.

'Look at her!' Joseph protested. 'She's just a child. I'm old enough to be her father! I'd be a laughing stock.'

The priest ignored all this, and the grumbles of the other men, and gave each of them a staff.

'Are we going somewhere?' asked Joachim. The staves were the sort of sticks they might use if they were going to walk a long way, or on uneven ground.

'Just hold them please,' said the priest. He stood back expectantly. Everyone waited.

'Is this going to take long?' asked Jacob.

'Yes, I've got customers waiting, you know,' said Joseph, who was getting quite ratty by now.

'Shhh …' said the priest. They waited and still nothing happened.

'What are we waiting for?' one of the men whispered.

'A sign,' whispered the priest.

'A sign?' asked Joseph. 'What kind of a sign?'

'I don't know,' admitted the priest. 'The Lord will choose Mary's husband.' Then silence settled.

After a while something most extraordinary happened, but afterwards no one could agree on what it was. Some said a flock of doves flew into the temple and settled on the staff Joseph was holding, and on his shoulders, and one even sat on his head. Others said that as Mary walked past the line of suitors the staff Joseph was holding suddenly burst forth leaves and blossomed beautiful flowers, like a branch on a tree in springtime.

In any case, it was clear that Joseph had been chosen.

'Thank you,' said the priest. 'The rest of you can go.'

Gratefully, they went, casting looks of commiseration and wonder towards Joseph.

Joseph felt trapped. 'I see,' he said angrily to the priest. (He ignored Mary, who was quite happy to be ignored: the whole procedure had been so embarrassing.) 'Mary needs a husband and Joseph will do — he's a nice bloke — steady job — you can't go wrong with Joseph.'

'Exactly,' said the priest, taking the wind out of Joseph's sails. 'You're a safe bet.'

'A safe bet?' spluttered Joseph. 'With a sixteen-year-old wife? Wake up! I'll be at work — my work takes me away from home a lot, you know — and she'll be "lonely". Who knows what she'll get up to? And I'll look a proper fool. I'm sorry, I'm not doing it.'

He thrust the staff into the priest's arms. 'And you can keep your magic stick!' he shouted, and stormed out of the Temple.

The priest calmly collected the staves and put them away, noticing that now that Joseph was no longer holding it, his stick looked just the same as all the others.

'And *that's* how Joseph and Mary got engaged,' said Red Hair.

'You see?' Green Beads said to the children, '... all part of a big plan.'

The Storyteller cleared his throat. 'May I?'

'Sorry,' said Green Beads, and told Red Hair to 'shhh'.

'Now this man Joseph, as we have said, was a carpenter, and he had to leave home straight after the betrothal for a job some miles away, leaving his young wife at home, alone ...'

There was a pleasant marketplace near Mary's house — more of a large courtyard really — with a fountain in the middle. When the sun shone, which it usually did, it was a good place to sit and spin, or sew, or play, and have a chat. Mary often met her friend Rebecca there. On this particular day some women were doing their washing in the fountain and their children were making mud pies.

Rebecca couldn't understand why Mary was making such a fuss about getting married. 'I wish someone would marry *me,*' she said.

'You're too young,' said Mary.

'I'm older than *you,*' said Rebecca.

'At least you'll get to choose who you marry,' complained Mary. 'You won't have to marry a stupid old carpenter. You won't have to marry someone who doesn't want to be married to you just as much as you don't want to be married to him.'

'My mum did,' said Rebecca.

'What's the matter with Mary?' one of the women asked her friends. 'She looks as though she's lost a shekel and found a lepton.' The other women laughed, because this was a very funny joke in those days.

'She's got a face like a fasting Pharisee,' said another, which made the women laugh even more, because this idea was also extremely amusing in those days.

'I've seen happier expressions on a camel's —'

'Ask her what's the matter,' the woman who was called Sarah quickly interrupted.

'Mary?' said the woman who was called Martha. 'Cheer up! He'll be back before you know it.' She of course assumed Mary was missing her new fiancé.

'I'm alright,' said Mary. 'I was just thinking, that's all.'

'Now listen here, Mary.' Sarah had evidently decided that Mary needed a good talking to. 'I know your Joseph may not be the youngest, handsomest, cleverest man in the world, but he's a good man, a solid man. You could do a lot worse.'

The other women, who all had husbands, warmly agreed.

'I know,' said Mary, still sounding far from happy.

'Look on the bright side,' said Martha. 'You'll never be short of furniture.'

Mary wandered a little way off, lost in her thoughts. 'It's just ... sometimes I wonder what it all means,' she said, to no one in particular. 'That business in the Temple ... It just seems so strange, that's all.'

What happened next, no one but Mary could tell. There were a number of people in the marketplace, yet no one saw or heard exactly what Mary felt.

Some said they saw an incredibly bright white light shining down on Mary from the sky, while others said a wind like a howling gale tugged at

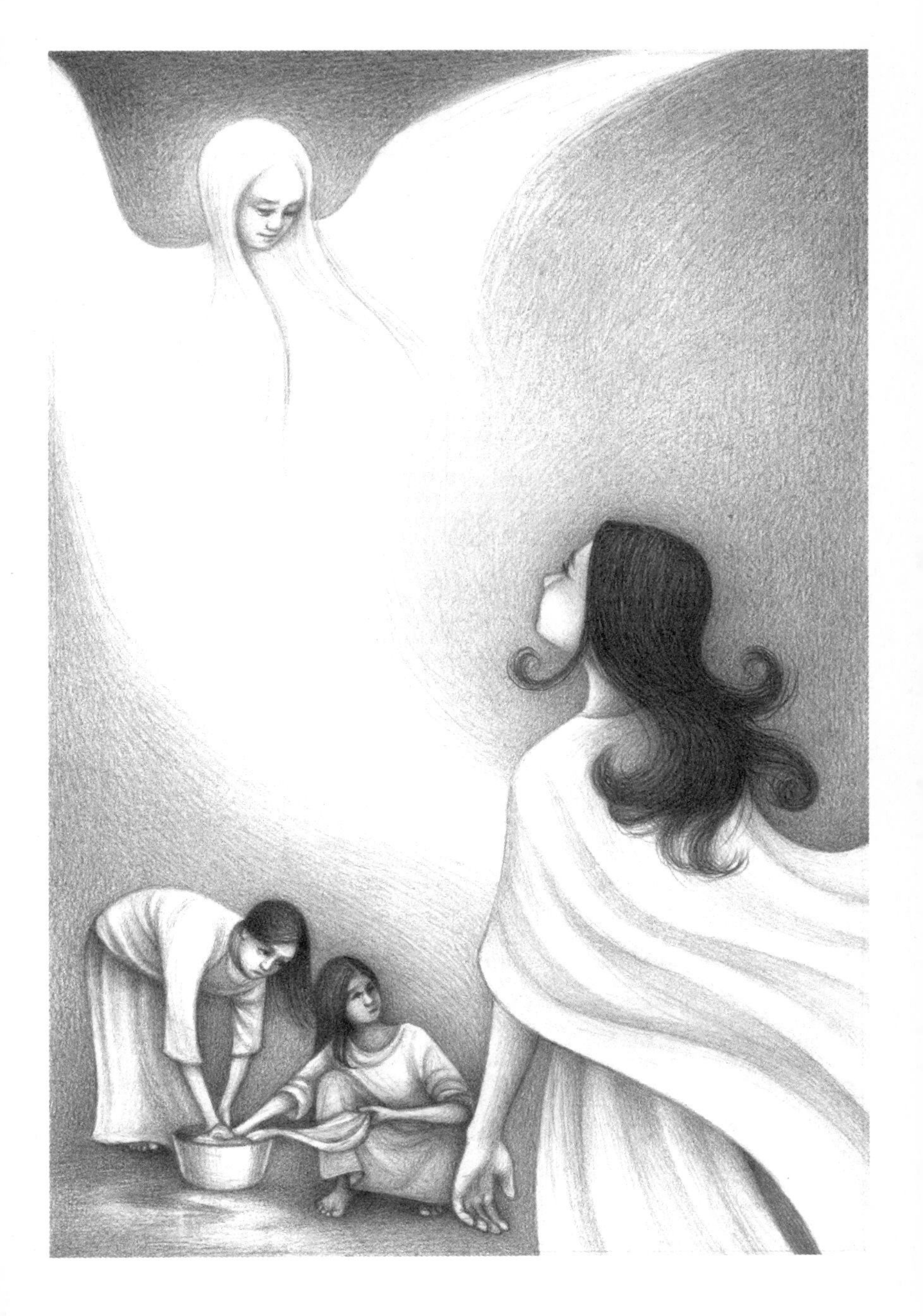

her clothes and hair but left everyone else undisturbed. All this while Mary seemed to be listening intently to something that no one else could hear. (Others admitted that they neither saw nor heard anything out of the ordinary.)

'Did you … did you see that?' she asked afterwards.

'What?' Martha and Sarah said together.

Mary didn't have the words to describe what had happened — perhaps such words don't exist. So she said: 'Nothing'.

But Sarah saw Mary was white as a sheet. 'What's the matter with you?' she asked. 'Are you alright?'

'Yes,' said Mary. 'It's just … I think I just saw …'

'What?' Martha demanded. 'What did you see?'

'An angel.' There. She'd said it.

The women stopped what they were doing and stared at Mary.

'The poor girl's exhausted,' one of them said eventually. 'It's been a long day.'

But the children were fascinated.

'Mary saw an angel!' cried one.

'Did you, Mary?' another asked excitedly.

'What did it look like?' The children all gathered round Mary, eager to know more.

'Give the poor girl some space,' said Martha. 'She didn't see any angel.'

'There's *no such thing,*' asserted Sarah.

But the children were not to be put off.

'Was it playing an instrument?' asked one.

'Did it fly?' asked another.

'Did it say anything?'

Mary did her best to explain the message she had received. 'I think I'm going to have a baby,' she said. 'A very special baby.'

The children cheered and danced around Mary, who didn't know whether to laugh or cry. But the women's faces were serious. They were wondering how on earth she was going to explain all this to Joseph.

'Joseph, I've got something to tell you,' Mary began. 'You see, there was this angel ...'

'That won't do,' said Rebecca. 'He'll think you've gone stark staring mad.'

The girls were finding it very difficult to come up with words which would help Joseph understand what had happened. Mary's mother was at the market and they were pacing about the kitchen, practising.

'I know,' said Mary. She stood up straight and threw back her shoulders. 'Joseph.'

'Excellent,' said Rebecca.

'Joseph. You remember all that business with the sticks or the staves or whatever they were at the Temple, and how nobody understood how it happened?'

'That's good!' said Rebecca, clapping her hands, 'much better!'

'Well ... something's happened to me that's also rather ...'

'Odd?' offered Rebecca. 'Mysterious? Inexplicable?'

'No, no!' said Mary in frustration.

'Try being more positive,' suggested Rebecca.

'Joseph!' Mary announced. 'Good news! I'm having a baby!'

'You're *what?*' Joseph was standing in the doorway.

Rebecca decided it was time to leave. She slipped past Joseph and ran all the way home.

'Isn't it … marvellous?' Mary struggled to sound cheerful. 'I'm having a baby!'

Joseph dropped his bag on the floor. 'But that's imposs …' His voice trailed away. He picked his bag up again. Then he put it down again. 'When did this happen?' he asked in a hollow voice, unfamiliar to Mary.

'While you were away,' said Mary.

'Where?'

'Just outside.'

'Outside?'

'In the marketplace.'

'In the marketplace?' Joseph's voice rose. 'What were you doing in the marketplace at night?'

'It wasn't night,' explained Mary. 'It was broad daylight. That's what was so strange.'

'Broad daylight!' Joseph looked as though he might explode. 'Have you no shame? If you were going to deceive me, did you have to do it in front of the whole world?' he shouted.

'I haven't deceived you!' Mary shouted back. 'And anyway, nobody else saw it.'

'Oh, that's alright then!' Joseph was being sarcastic. 'They'll soon know, though, won't they? When they see poor old Joseph and his fat wife.' He sat down at the table and put his head in his hands. After a few moments he spoke in a calm, but still angry voice. 'Who is he, then?'

'Who?' said Mary.

'The father! The man in the marketplace!'

'There was no man in the marketplace!' said Mary. 'It was ... an angel,' she added quietly.

Joseph thought he couldn't have heard her properly. 'I beg your pardon?'

'An angel!' Mary cried. 'It was an angel!'

'Good grief,' said Joseph to himself. 'She's gone stark staring mad.' He thought for a moment. 'Did he look anything like a Roman, this 'angel'?'

Mary sat down at the table and burst into tears. That was all Joseph needed. 'I'm the one who should be crying!' he shouted. 'I'm the one who's marrying a pregnant mad person! If I could lay my hands on that priest and his magic stick now ... I *knew* something like this would happen. Everyone always said you were *special.*' And, as he said the word, it occurred to Joseph that Mary just might be telling the truth. Could this be part of the big plan? He began to wonder.

'You just don't understand,' Mary sobbed.

Joseph sighed. 'No, I don't understand.'

'I didn't choose it! I didn't choose any of it!' Mary said.

'I know,' Joseph said in a softer voice. 'Neither did I.'

Mary stood up suddenly. 'I hate being special!' she said. 'I hate being good! And I hate you!' And she ran out, slamming the door behind her.

'Just tell her you'll *be there*. You'll *be there* for

her,' Joachim suggested. Joseph had come to his friend's shop for some advice about how to make it up with Mary.

'Be where?' asked Joseph. 'Where will I be?'

Joachim threw the piece of leather he was cutting down on the table in frustration. Sometimes Joseph could be very dim indeed. 'Wherever she is! Tell her you'll support her, you'll look after her. You'll try and understand this special thing that's happening … this special baby.'

'I can't. I'm no good with words. I'm a carpenter. I make things. Out of wood.'

'Try!'

Joseph cleared his throat. 'Mary,' he began rehearsing. 'Mary, I'm sorry. I'm no good with words. I'm just a carpenter. But I want you to know, I'd like to make you things. Anything you like. As long as it's out of wood.' He cleared his throat again. 'What do you think?'

There was a silence.

'Are you talking to me or Mary?' Joachim asked.

'You. Well, what do you think?'

Joachim tried to think of what to say. 'I don't think it's quite ready yet.'

'She won't see me, anyway. She hates me.'

'She's probably just upset,' said Joachim.

'She doesn't realize that *I'm* upset too!' Joseph burst out. 'She doesn't seem to understand how bad this looks. Why can't she go away quietly somewhere and have the baby? Everyone will know I'm not the father. It's so … embarrassing.'

Joachim sighed. 'Look at this sandal, Joseph,'

he said, holding up one he had finished making. 'Imagine it's Mary's.'

'Her feet aren't that big!' protested Joseph.

'*Imagine!* Now think about wearing her sandals.'

'They wouldn't fit me,' said Joseph.

'*Imagine!* I mean, think about what it must be like being Mary. Look at all this from her point of view. She's just a girl. She's been given this huge, confusing, frightening responsibility. That's a bit harder to deal with than feeling embarrassed.'

Joseph was ashamed. 'You mean you have to be in someone else's shoes — to see life as they see it — and I haven't been doing that. I've just been thinking about myself.'

'Exactly.'

Joseph picked up his bag of tools. 'Thank you, Joachim. I know what I've got to do now.'

'Good. Good luck old mate.'

'I'm going to make her something,' Joseph said as he went out of the door.

'Out of wood?' asked Joachim. But Joseph had gone, happily whistling down the street.

'Nine months later ...' continued the Storyteller.

'Wait a minute,' said one of the children who had been listening. 'What happened to Mary and Joseph? Did they make up?'

'You'll see,' said the Storyteller. 'Just listen ...'

'What did he make for her?' asked another child.

'I don't know,' said the Storyteller. 'It's not important.'

'I bet it was a cradle,' another said, 'for the baby.'

'Or a rattle. Babies like rattles. My little sister ...'

'If people would just stop interrupting me, I might be able to get on,' said the Storyteller firmly.

When everyone was quiet again, he went on. 'Nine months later ...'

The marketplace was thronging with people. Joseph was helping Mary with the shopping, as the baby was due to be born soon and she got tired easily. A beating drum and shouting heralded the arrival of some Roman soldiers. People stepped resentfully aside as the soldiers pushed through the crowd. Marcus climbed some steps in front of a house and the other soldiers lined up below him, facing the disgruntled citizens. Marcus signalled to the drummer to be quiet and unrolled a scroll of paper.

'People of Nazareth!' he addressed the crowd, in his loud foreign accent. 'Hear and take due notice of a communication from your Emperor ...'

His words were drowned out by people booing and complaining loudly. His soldiers took a step forward and there was instant silence.

'... your Emperor Caesar Augustus, in Rome.' Pleased to have their full attention, he cleared his throat. 'The Emperor has issued a decree, that the most comprehensive census ever undertaken is to be carried out, one week from now, in which all will participate by proceeding to their city of origin, accompanied by their whole families ...'

Again his words became inaudible as people started arguing and heckling. His soldiers banged their spears on the ground in a threatening fashion and there was quiet again.

'No exceptions!' said Marcus. '... where they will co-operate with the Roman Imperial authorities in answering all relevant questions pertaining to the composition of their household, the value of their assets, *et cetera, et cetera, et cetera.*' He rolled up the decree. 'The long and the short of which is that *all the world is to be taxed.*' He started to descend the stairs.

'All the world is to be taxed?' shouted Joachim. 'Who does the Emperor think he is? God?'

'Yes, as a matter of fact,' answered Marcus.

'Why should we be taxed?' shouted Martha.

'Absolutely!' agreed Sarah. 'What have the Romans ever done for us?'

'This is outrageous!' said Jacob.

'My wife's going to have a baby any day now,' called out Joseph. 'She can't possibly travel!'

'No exceptions,' Marcus replied, and turned to speak to his men.

'I've a good mind to make a formal complaint,' Jacob announced.

'Please refer any queries to my office at the regional governor's residence — King Herod's palace — in Jerusalem,' Marcus said, preparing to leave.

'I wouldn't bother, mate,' one of the soldiers muttered to Jacob.

'Hail Caesar!' cried Marcus, saluting.

'Hail Caesar!' the soldiers answered, saluting.

Marcus jumped up on the edge of the fountain so he could be seen and surveyed the people.

'I *said* "Hail Caesar",' he said in a cold voice.

The people in the crowd half-heartedly mumbled 'Hail Caesar' but would not return Marcus's salute. At Marcus's signal the drumming began again and the Romans departed.

'There's no need to push!' said Mary, as the soldiers jostled past her. One of them stopped dead in his tracks, with a strange expression on his face. 'Sorry, my lady,' he said. 'I didn't realize ...' But when he turned to her, Mary had gone.

'Our story now takes us to Bethlehem, one week later,' said the Storyteller. 'The little town was inundated with families coming to register themselves in the census. Every living person who had ever been born there poured through the streets; cold, tired and hungry; the young helped the old, the healthy carried the sick; no exceptions ...'

As night fell, the streets emptied. Some people were staying with their relations, but even many of these had to sleep on the floor. Others had filled up the inns or brought tents. Joseph had tried everywhere, but there was not a spare bed to be found in the whole of Bethlehem. Finally an innkeeper who had even given up his own bed for an old man who couldn't walk took one look at Mary and said, 'Come with me.' He led them down a little dark alley and pushed open a door.

He hung his lantern on a nail and Mary and Joseph could see pairs of bright eyes glinting in the light. The air was full of the warm smell of animals and fresh hay.

'It's not much,' apologized the innkeeper, 'but you can't sleep in the street, not in her condition.'

Mary had already lain down on the soft hay, exhausted. Joseph thanked the innkeeper who shut the door quietly behind him. He had left his lantern inside, in case the young couple needed it in the night, but realized he could see quite well without it. Looking up at the night sky he was amazed to see a very bright star with a long tail like a comet, right above his stable, and wondered why he had not noticed it before.

'Of course,' said the Storyteller, 'some people had no difficulty finding lodgings in Bethlehem …'

The sound of laughter filled the room Marcus and his soldiers had commandeered for the night. The men were gathered round the fire, drinking the local wine and playing dice, while Marcus sat in the corner, cleaning his sword. The door opened and a rush of cold air came in with the soldier. Marcus looked up. 'Did you find them?' he asked.

'Yes, sir,' the soldier replied. 'The magi have set up camp on the outskirts of the town. They haven't found the prince yet. But I did learn something else about him.'

'Oh yes?' Marcus put down his sword. 'What's that?'

'It seems that the one we're looking for is a baby.'

The other soldiers fell silent.

'We haven't got to kill a baby, have we, sir?' one of them asked.

'We'll follow our orders, whatever they are,' Marcus snapped sharply. 'Anyway, we've got to find him first.' Marcus considered the best course of action. He beckoned the soldier who had brought the news and took him into a private corner.

'Ride back to Jerusalem as fast as you can,' he said. 'Explain this baby business to King Herod. He might want to reconsider.'

Joseph banged on the door as hard as he could. The innkeeper had directed him to the house. 'Hello! Hello!' shouted Joseph. 'I need a midwife! It's really quite urgent!'

Finally a light appeared at an upstairs window. Moments later a face looked out. 'Alright, alright, I'm coming.' It took what seemed like an eternity for the woman to come to the door, pulling on her apron. 'How far apart are the pains?' she asked, rubbing her eyes.

'Oh, pretty frequent, really quite urgent, if you'll just come …' Joseph was pulling her along the street. 'You see, she's having a baby!'

'You don't say!' the midwife yawned.

'Yes,' said Joseph, 'and it's a very special baby —'

'Yes, dear,' soothed the midwife, slowing him down. 'Your first time, is it?'

'It's a very special boy —'

'Yes, dear,' said the midwife, detaching his hand from her apron, 'a boy. Although if it's a girl we'll be just as pleased, won't we?'

'But it isn't a girl; it's a boy,' stated Joseph. 'It's all part of a big plan.'

'I see,' said the midwife. 'A big plan.'

'No, you don't, and I don't blame you,' said Joseph. 'I didn't understand it at first; in fact I still don't understand it if I'm honest. You see, we didn't even … I mean … it just happened.'

The midwife stopped walking and took a long cool look at Joseph. 'No. Now you've lost me.'

'There was this angel, apparently.' Joseph led her through the little alley to the stable. 'This is the place.' He was about to go in when the midwife, gently but firmly, pulled him back.

'Alright, lovey,' she said. 'Now you get back to your wine and your angel. This is women's work.'

'Oh, I see,' said Joseph. 'I'll be off, then.'

The midwife opened the door.

'Are you sure you don't want me to do anything?' Joseph asked.

'I think you've done quite enough already, don't you?' said the midwife, and shooed him away. 'Off you go.'

And off Joseph went, leaving Mary under the kind care of the midwife, the gentle gaze of the animals and the bright beacon in the sky.

Back in Jerusalem, Herod was surprised to see the soldier.

'Aren't you supposed to be in Bethlehem?' he asked.

'I have an urgent message from Commander Marcus, King Herod.'

'Good news, I hope?' asked Herod.

'This upstart prince we're after. The troublemaker. Turns out it's a baby, sir. And we don't know which one. Bethlehem's full of babies, sir.'

'Then kill them all,' said Herod simply, and walked towards the door.

'Kill *all* the babies, sir?' the soldier asked.

'No!' said Herod, pausing in front of a mirror. He adjusted his robe. 'Just the boys.'

'Meanwhile,' the Storyteller continued, 'while Bethlehem slept, in the hills around the little town there were shepherds abiding in their field, keeping watch over their flocks by night ...'

'Never in all my years out on these hills have I ever seen a star so bright,' said Zebedee. 'Never seen anything like it.'

Zebedee and Aaron were staring up at the extraordinary star that had appeared in the sky over Bethlehem.

'Do you think it's a significant omen?' asked Aaron.

'No,' said Zebedee. 'That's definitely a star.'

'No, I mean, do you think it's a portent of salvation? An emblem of hope? A *sign?*'

Zebedee gave this some thought before concluding: 'No. I think you'll find that's just a star. Big one, mind you. That star's bigger than Peter's house.'

'Bigger than his house *and* his stable,' added Aaron.

'Ar,' agreed Zebedee. (Over years of living on the hills, this sound, meaning 'yes' had become indistinguishable from the bleats of the sheep.)

'Bigger than his house and his stable *and* that little lean-to bit on the side,' added Aaron.

'I don't know about *that* ...' Zebedee said.

They were still staring at the star like statues, resting their chins on their crooks, when Isaac returned a little while later. 'Sheep alright, then?' asked Zebedee.

'Ar,' said Isaac. 'What do you make of that star then?'

'We was just saying, wasn't we?' said Aaron.

'Ar,' said Zebedee. 'It's a big 'un alright.'

They all contemplated for a while. They spent a lot of their time doing this, and were used to long periods of nothing happening.

'Town's full of people tonight,' Isaac said some time later. 'Crawling with 'em. And Romans. Can't move for Romans. All talking in ... what do you call it? Roman! Nonsense I call it.'

Zebedee chuckled. 'And they reckon us shepherds are not "noted for our conversation!"'

The other two agreed.

'Next to them, we're philosophers, we are,' said Aaron.

Then no one said anything for quite a while, except for 'sheep alright, then?' and 'ar'.

'Then there's their numbers,' said Isaac.

Zebedee nudged Aaron. 'He only says that because he can only count up to V!'

'X!' protested Isaac. 'I can count up to X!'

'I counted up to L once,' said Aaron. Zebedee and Isaac were duly impressed and they all fell silent for some minutes wondering just how many L was, and whether they had more or less than L sheep.

'And their geography isn't up to much, either,' said Aaron.

'Too right,' Zebedee warmly agreed.

'How'd you mean?' asked Isaac.

'*All roads lead to Rome,*' said Zebedee. 'That can't be right, can it? *All roads lead to Rome*. I mean, take this road. Where does it lead to?'

'Bethlehem, of course,' said Isaac.

'Ah,' said Aaron, 'but where does it lead to the *other* way?'

'Peter's house,' Isaac said, some time later.

'See what I mean?' Zebedee said triumphantly. 'How they've managed to conquer the world is beyond me. How did they ever manage to leave Rome in the first place? According to *their* logic, the road out of town would have taken them straight back to Rome again.'

'How do you reckon they got here, then?' Aaron wondered.

'I dunno,' admitted Zebedee. 'Perhaps they got lost.'

'Ar,' said Isaac.

Aaron fetched a great sigh. 'Do you ever wonder,' he began, 'what the *point* of it all is?'

The other two shepherds looked at him.

'I mean to say,' he went on, 'is life all just eat, sleep and sheep? Every day just eat, sleep and sheep; eat, sleep and sheep; eat, sleep and sheep; and sometimes — just for a bit of variety — having a pop at the Romans?'

The other two shepherds looked at each other.

'What's wrong with that, then?' asked Zebedee.

'I'm not saying there's anything wrong with it,'

Aaron was quick to assure him. 'But sometimes, don't you wish something ... *exciting* would happen?'

'Like what?' asked Isaac. 'Like a travelling circus?'

'No, he doesn't mean that, do you?' said Zebedee. 'You mean something *really* exciting, like ... like a sheep having triplets.'

'Piglets?' asked Aaron, suddenly excited.

'*Triplets*. They call that "a blessing" — when a sheep has triplets. That would be exciting, wouldn't it?'

'Yes, of course,' said Aaron, 'but I mean ... Oh, I don't know what I mean really. Perhaps I'll go and check on the sheep.'

And Aaron went to check on the sheep.

All of a sudden Zebedee and Isaac heard singing. It wasn't just one voice, but as if all the hills around them were full of invisible choirs. At the same time a blinding light shone on them, so bright that they had to shield their eyes with their hands. They clung to each other for fear of being somehow carried off by the musical brightness which seemed too powerful to resist. They could almost make out the shape of a person of some kind, but he, or she, seemed made of light, and did not stand on the ground but was above them, in the sky. They began to understand the words in the singing: it was a message straight from heaven to *them*. Then all of a sudden, they opened their eyes to find they were alone in the dark on the hillside; the only sound they could hear was the gentle bleating of the sheep; the only

brightness in the sky was from the great star. They were both in a state of shock, but also inexplicably happy.

'Did you hear ...?' began Isaac.

'I did,' said Zebedee.

'Did you see ...?'

'I did,' said Zebedee. He swallowed. 'They do have wings, then.'

'What do you reckon we should do?' asked Isaac.

'We'd better get going!' said Zebedee. 'We'd better find that baby! We'd better spread the word! Come on.'

At that moment Aaron returned. 'Sheep are alright,' he said.

'Never mind the sheep, we've got to get to Bethlehem,' Isaac told him. 'We're on a mission from God!' He and Zebedee began to hurry down the road to Bethlehem.

'Wait a minute!' Aaron called. 'What's going on? Don't tell me I missed something exciting!' He hurried after them.

'We're *not* to be afraid,' Zebedee informed him. 'He was most emphatic on that point.'

'Who?'

'The angel — good tidings — great joy,' Isaac explained hurriedly, 'Saviour — born today — lying in a manger.'

'Lots of singing,' added Zebedee. 'What did they sing?'

'Glory to God in the highest,' Isaac repeated, *'and on earth peace, goodwill to all men.'*

'What? Even to the Romans?' Aaron asked. 'Wait a minute, hadn't one of us better stay with the sheep?'

'They'll be alright,' said Isaac, breaking into a run. 'From now on, everything's going to be alright!'

'The shepherds followed the star all the way to the stable,' said the Storyteller, 'where they found Mary and Joseph and the new born baby, just as the angel had ...'

'Excuse me,' said one of the children, 'but how did Joseph know the baby had been born?'

'Yes,' said another, ' the midwife told him to go away.'

'That's a very good point,' said Red Hair, before the Storyteller could answer, 'because while the shepherds were seeing the angel, Joseph saw something strange too.'

'In another part of the hills above Bethlehem,' Green Beads began, 'Joseph was walking, wondering how Mary was, and how long it would be before the baby was born, and whether everything would be alright, when *suddenly* ...'

... Joseph realized he walked, and yet did not walk. At that moment, a great silence descended. Even the wind stopped: there was no breeze. There was no movement of the corn in the fields, the leaves on the trees, nor was the sound of water heard.

The brooks did not babble, the rivers did not flow, the waves on the sea were frozen as they crested. The birds did not fly, but hung motionless in the sky, as in a picture. The goats stood by the pool, their tongues in the water, but did not drink.

At that moment, the whole world stood still.

And then, suddenly, everything went on its course.

'Anyway,' said the Storyteller. 'The shepherds followed the star all the way to the stable, where they found Mary and Joseph and the new born baby, just as the angel had …'

'Excuse me,' said one of the children, 'but what happened to the midwife?'

'Yes,' said another, 'if it was such a special baby …'

'Well, it's funny you should say that,' said Green Beads.

The Storyteller sighed.

The child himself, like the sun, shone brightly, most beautiful and delightful to see. It seemed to the midwife as if he were peace itself, bringing peace everywhere. The stable was filled with light, brighter than the sun, and there was a most sweet smell.

The midwife stood stupefied and amazed. Fear had seized her. She was transfixed, gazing at the intense bright light which had been born. She watched as the light gradually shrank and began to take the shape of a baby. She became braver and leaned over and touched him. She then lifted him into her arms with great awe, and was astonished because he seemed weightless, not like other newborn babies.

She examined him carefully. He was perfect, but his whole body was shining. He was *light* to carry, *radiant* to see.

She was amazed at him because he didn't cry, as most newborn babies do. While she held him in her arms, looking into his face, he smiled at her with a most joyful smile, and, opening his eyes, he looked at her intently, and suddenly a great light came forth from his eyes, like a brilliant flash of lightning.

The shepherds were not the new baby's first visitors. The midwife had wrapped him up and laid him in the manger, where the animals watched over him with quiet interest. Joseph and Mary couldn't take their eyes off him — it was clear that he was indeed a very special baby. The magi were the first to arrive. As soon as they came into the stable, they knelt, as if before a king. Then they gave Mary and Joseph the rich gifts they had carried so far: gold, frankincense and myrrh. They looked at the new baby with wonder and joy and smiled and wept.

Then Balthazar took Joseph aside and spoke to him very seriously. He explained that the tiny baby already had enemies. Herod's soldiers had followed them to Bethlehem intending to find and kill the child. Joseph's eyes filled with tears as he looked at Mary smiling over the little boy.

'How can I save him?' he asked Balthazar.

Balthazar beckoned Caspar and Melchior over, and Melchior showed Joseph a map. They had worked out a safe route for Mary and Joseph to get home. Instead of going back to Nazareth by the shortest way they were to go through Egypt. The magi would do their best to throw the soldiers off the scent and give Mary, Joseph and the baby time to escape to safety. The most dangerous part would be getting out of Bethlehem itself.

A soft knock at the door startled them all. Mary held the baby close.

'May we come in?' asked a voice. 'We've come to see the baby.'

Caspar opened the door a crack and when he saw it was just three shepherds he let them in. The shepherds approached the manger and, as the magi had done, knelt down. After a while Zebedee, who had suddenly become very shy, said: 'I … er … we have no rich gifts … it was rather short notice … and anyway … we couldn't afford … we brought you this.' He offered Mary a sheepskin for the baby.

'And our love,' said Aaron.

'Yes, and our love,' said Isaac.

Mary thanked them and wrapped the infant in the soft white wool.

'How did you get here?' asked Melchior.

'Angel,' said Aaron. 'You?'

'Star,' said Caspar. And everybody laughed.

Suddenly Aaron put his fingers to his lips. They all fell silent. There was some kind of noise in the street outside. As it got louder they could hear it was a terrible and frightening noise — men shouting and women screaming, people running and babies crying. They listened hard, trying to make out what they were shouting. When the words came, they were full of fear and panic: 'Run! Run for your lives!' one cried. 'Take your children and run!' screamed another. 'The Romans are killing the children!' a woman wailed, horrible to hear.

Soon the streets were deserted. Everyone had hidden, run away or been murdered as they tried to protect their children. But the Roman soldiers had not given up. They continued to search house after house, looking for the baby boy they had been ordered to kill.

Mary and Joseph hurried through narrow passages and alleys to the outskirts of the town. As they emerged into a courtyard they stopped dead. A Roman soldier was standing right in front of them. He had his back to them and was staring up at the star which continued to blaze brightly in the night sky. Though they were absolutely still and silent, something made him turn round.

'What have you got there?' he said in a rough voice, drawing his sword.

Mary and Joseph were frozen to the spot, terrified. The soldier reached out and pulled back the sheepskin the baby was wrapped in. He looked long and hard at the baby.

'Go,' he said eventually, in a gentle voice.

Mary and Joseph were too scared to move.

'Go!' he repeated and raised his sword. 'Go now!'

He watched as Mary and Joseph hurried away through the shadows, and was still staring after them long after they had vanished from view.

'Soldier!' called Marcus, as he entered the courtyard. 'What are you doing? Found anything? What's keeping you?'

The soldier turned to Marcus. 'Nothing, sir. It was nothing,' he said. 'I just saw a star, sir. The brightest star I've ever seen. That's all.'

Green Beads wiped her eyes. 'Joseph and Mary, on the magi's advice, made their escape into Egypt for the baby's safety.'

'And, as they crossed the desert,' Red Hair continued, 'they saw lions and panthers and all kinds of fierce wild animals approaching them, and they were very afraid.'

'But then,' said Green Beads, 'they realized that the wild animals came not to attack them, but to escort them through the wilderness and guard them.'

'They walked among wolves and feared nothing.'

'And the lions directed them in their path.'

The story over, those who had been listening were getting up ready to leave when a little girl came running. She made her way through the crowd of people to the Storyteller. 'Sorry I'm late. Have I missed it?'

'I'm afraid you have,' said the Storyteller, 'but don't worry. We'll tell it again next year.'

'I can't wait until then!' she said. 'What happened?'

'Well, there was an angel …' began one child.

'And a star,' added another.

'A king and some soldiers, magi …'

'They're wise men …'

'And some shepherds …'

'So, how did it end?' asked the girl.

'With a baby being born,' another answered.

'That's not much of an ending!' she protested.

'Oh, it's not the end,' explained the Storyteller, as he came out from under the shade of the great tree, blinking in the bright sunshine. 'It's just the beginning.'

Sources

The story of the nativity as it is usually known is based on an amalgamation of the accounts found in the opening chapters of the gospels of Matthew and Luke. Their versions differ in several ways: for example, only Matthew gives us the magi and only Luke gives us the shepherds. This retelling also draws on extra-biblical legends and apocrypha which early Christians read. Joseph's experience of the world standing still is adapted from the Protevangelium of James; the midwife's experience of the birth is from Arundel 404. Accounts of Mary's early life, Joseph's background and the methods by which he was chosen as Mary's husband, all appear in similar texts. Medieval accounts frequently emphasize both the miraculous and the everyday — particularly in presenting Joseph and Mary as flawed mortals with ordinary preoccupations. Medieval drama often used the shepherd scene or play as a comedy vehicle. As a general rule, the Storyteller gives the authorized version of the nativity story, while the women who interrupt him tell the tales which did not find their way into the New Testament.

Gunhild Sehlin, *Mary's Little Donkey and the Flight to Egypt*

The stubborn, dirty little donkey who is of no use to anyone in Nazareth becomes a quick and willing helper under Mary's care. The other animals in Mary's stable like him and together they wait for the birth of Mary's child.

But Mary and Joseph have to leave Nazareth obeying Caesar's decree, and the donkey carries Mary to Bethlehem where the child is born.

The donkey hopes to carry Mary and her son quickly back to Nazareth, but instead they have to flee to faraway Egypt.

An engaging Christmas story for young children.

Floris Books

Margaret Forrester, *The Cat Who Decided*

Based on the real story of a family cat who came “free” with an Edinburgh house, this is an ideal read-aloud, told with gentle humour and genuine respect for a cat who was very special. — *Lindsey Fraser, Sunday Herald*

The little stripey cat is on a journey. He is sent from the farm to the city and passed from owner to owner.

Once he moves to Edinburgh and finds his name — Mac — life gets more interesting.

Then, just when he starts to feel settled, unsettling things start to happen. Will he ever find someone to love him for always?

Young Kelpies

Kathleen Fidler, *Flash the Sheep Dog*

Tom Stokes is an orphan. His sister is going to America to get married, but where can he go? They remember an uncle and aunt they scarcely know who live in the borders of Scotland.

After the city bustle of London, Tom finds his uncle's farm barren and lonely. Help comes in the form of a sheepdog pup, and his loneliness is forgotten when Tom realizes it is his, to love and to train (maybe to be a champion?). Life on the hill-farm, with his new friend Elspeth, and Flash, becomes adventurous and challenging.

Young Kelpies